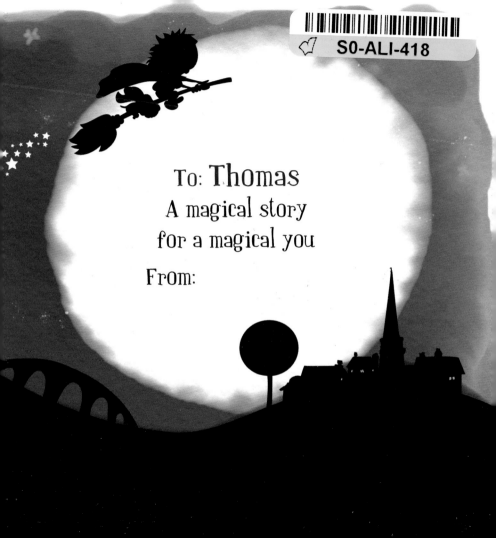

To: Thomas
A magical story
for a magical you

From:

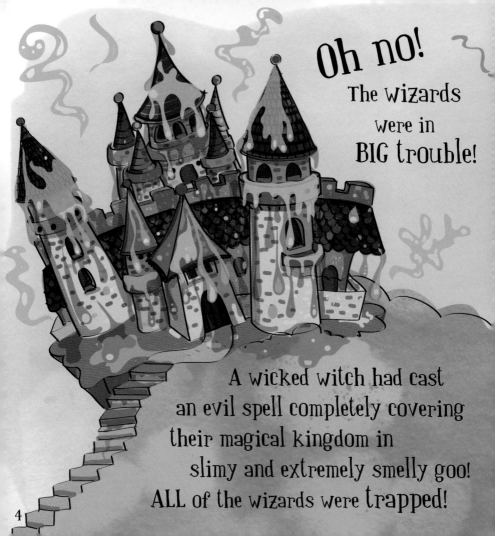

Oh no!
The wizards
were in
BIG trouble!

A wicked witch had cast
an evil spell completely covering
their magical kingdom in
slimy and extremely smelly goo!
ALL of the wizards were trapped!

4

The wizards really needed
someone to help them catch
the wicked witch,
but **who?**

5

The wise old grand wizard looked through his special telescope, and spotted someone who might just be able to help them.

"Quickly! Send Magical Master Owl to ask for Thomas's help in saving us from the wicked witch!" shouted the wizard.

6

Magical Master Owl knew he had
to help so he flapped and fluttered
as swiftly as he could to find the boy
spotted through the telescope.

"WHIZZ BAM !"

Thomas said, as he waved his pretend wand towards his dog Ruffles.

"Oh Ruffles you are supposed to turn into a flying dog."

Thomas SO wanted to be a Wizard.

8

Suddenly
with a flitter and
a flap, Magical
Master Owl
squawked through Thomas's
window into the bedroom and
explained (in his best owlish) the
trouble the wizards were in, and
asked a shocked Thomas
if he could help.

"Of course!"
said a delighted Thomas.

So Magical Master Owl squawked
three times, flapped his wings
four times, and with a WHIZZ
PUFF, a broomstick, cape and
magic wand suddenly appeared!

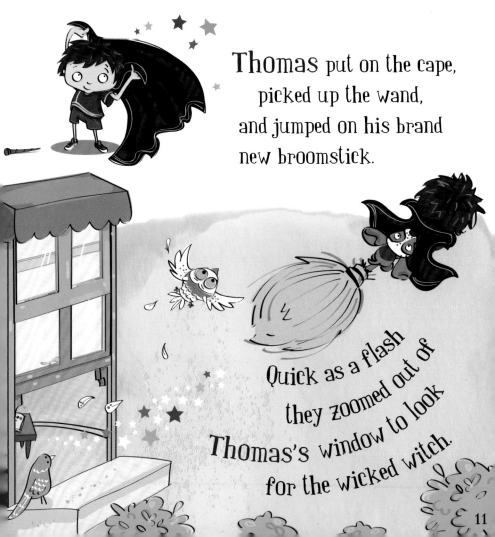

Thomas put on the cape,
picked up the wand,
and jumped on his brand
new broomstick.

Quick as a flash
they zoomed out of
Thomas's window to look
for the wicked witch.

11

The wicked witch was flying around, covering everything and everyone with her yucky, smelly green goo.

"Wahahaha!" she cackled, "Soon the whole world will be covered in my smelly goo and there are no wizards here to stop me!"

But little did she realize that **Thomas** was on his way.

He zoomed under bridges...

...and over houses, looking for the goo-spreading witch.

13

Suddenly Ruffles made
a big booming **bark**.
His super-smelling nose had caught
a whiff of the wicked witch, but she
was too far away for Thomas
to cast a spell on her.

14

Thomas clicked
his heels, gripped his
broomstick even tighter,
and zoomed at supersonic speed
towards the wicked witch.

15

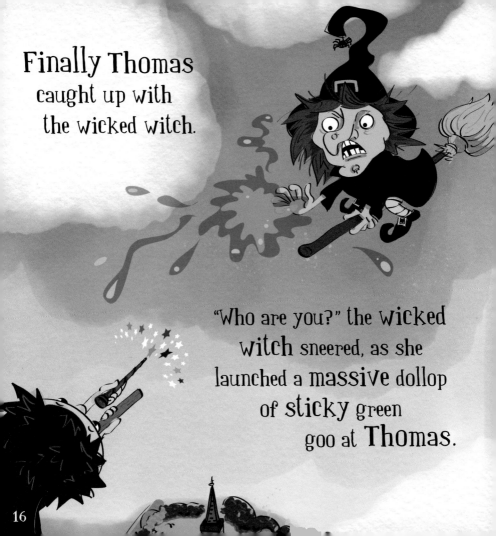

Finally Thomas caught up with the wicked witch.

"Who are you?" the wicked witch sneered, as she launched a **massive** dollop of **sticky** green goo at Thomas.

16

With lightning speed
Thomas waved his magic wand.
"BIZZ POP GOO I will stop you!" he shouted.
A huge brightly-colored umbrella appeared,
deflecting all of the smelly goo.

17

The wicked witch squealed
with anger, zapping another
dollop of smelly green goo
towards Thomas.

"WHIZZ SPLAT
send me your hat!"
Thomas shouted.

The witch's hat flew off
her head, catching all of her
smelly green goo. Yuck!

The witch couldn't
believe what this boy
wizard was doing!

18

"ZIP ZAP, you will be
trapped in your hat!"
Thomas cast another spell.

The witch's goo-filled hat
flew back to her,
squashing down
over her head,
squishing
her in the
smelly
green goo.

Hurray the wicked witch was trapped!

A triumphant **Thomas** took the wicked witch back to the wizards' castle.

All the slippery, slimy green goo had now gone thanks to **Thomas** breaking the bad witch's horrible spell.

20

The wizards were so grateful to
Thomas that they let him keep the cape,
broomstick AND magic wand!

Thomas finally felt like a true wizard!

The End

COLOR ME IN

_____'S
BOOK OF
SPELLS